LITTLE PILLS

Melody Dodds

An imprint of Enslow Publishing

WEST **44** BOOKS™

Please visit our website, www.west44books.com.
For a free color catalog of all our high-quality books,
call toll free 1-800-542-2595 or fax 1-877-542-2596.

Cataloging-in-Publication Data

Names: Dodds, Melody.
Title: Little pills / Melody Dodds.
Description: New York : West 44, 2019. | Series: West 44 YA verse
Identifiers: ISBN 9781538382813 (pbk.) | ISBN 9781538382820 (library
bound) | ISBN 9781538383414 (ebook)
Subjects: LCSH: Children's poetry, American. | Children's poetry, English. |
English poetry.
Classification: LCC PS586.3 L588 2019 | DDC 811'.60809282--dc23

First Edition

Published in 2019 by
Enslow Publishing LLC
101 West 23rd Street, Suite #240
New York, NY 10011

Editor: Caitie McAneney
Designer: Sam DeMartin

Photo Credits: Cover BSIP/UIG/Universal Images Group/Getty Images.

Printed in the United States of America

CPSIA compliance information: Batch #CS18W44: For further information contact
Enslow Publishing LLC, New York, New York at 1-800-542-2595.

FOR THE TOUGH KIDS, AND THE LONELY KIDS, AND ESPECIALLY
FOR THOSE WHO ARE BOTH.

THE SCULPTOR

They say
meth
is   the Monster.

Well.

Oxy   is
an artist who
sculpts
the monster
out of

                                            you.

ESCAPE

The bathroom
is the only place in this house
where I am *guaranteed*
privacy.

So I tend
to spend a

L

O

N

G

time in here.

Let's be clear: I mean "house" in the sense of
home.

House really means
apartment.

Three bedrooms, one bath.
Five people…no, wait.

Four.
Still—
do the math.

Let's be clear: I mean "privacy" in the sense of
walls.

Privacy barely means
solitude.

Someone always needs to use it.

Stay in too long
and they lose it.

But here I am.

No pounding yet
from my mother or
her husband, Rupert.

And no threats
from my sister, Isabella,
who is younger
but whose hunger
to hurt me
is a thing I can't forget.

So I escape.

SAFE

Looking at the mirror
but really
through it.

Messing with my hair
but thinking
of a boy.

Glossing my lips
(for the same boy)
but waiting for
                    changing leaves
                    flannel shirts
                    pumpkins
                    cider
                    fires
            HALLOWEEN!
                    candy

and

bam bam bam

GET OUTTA THERE!

(My sister.)

THE COOLEST GIRL SHE'S EVER SEEN

I make myself
MEAN.

I
squint.

I
scowl.

I throw open the bathroom door
and growl
words I should not say.

(But Mom's away.)

Surprise!
Outside the door
is not my sister anymore.

Instead
some other girl her age.

Still,
I fill with rage,
and stomp away.

But
as I do
I hear this stranger say,

Your sister

is

soooo...

pretty.

She's,

like,

the

coolest

girl

I've

ever

seen.

ISABELLA DISAGREES

Cool?!?!?

How about:
      rude
      mean
      selfish
      nasty
      cruel.

Monster tomboy who:
        lies
        steals
        sneaks around
        does things she's told
        not to.

She's failing school!

She's horrible. She's SCARY !

If you lived with her,

you'd see.

You can't think
my sister's
  cool

and still be friends with me.

MY BROTHER'S ROOM

My older brother,
Leopold.

My brother
who is
gone.

Not like my mother,
who just works too much.
Leo's physically
moved on.

He doesn't live here
anymore.

But all his stuff
still does.

Which makes me sad
but
sometimes
happy.

Because:

he locked his room
before he left
but left
his window cracked
enough that I can sneak in.

Like some big,
yellow-haired
rat.

But I don't want
anyone else
to know.

So
I say
I'm going out
then break
back in
to
my own home.

Slip through that crack
by
standing tiptoed
on a can
filled with
trash.

Push it wide
and step through
to a room
that's like a tomb.

Or I guess
like
a memorial.

Then I do
this thing

I do
sometimes,

more often
lately.

Where I take
this pill I took
from Gramma

and
I let it
just
sedate me.

MY BROTHER

My older brother,
Leopold—

my brother
who is
gone—

was the fifth of us.

I forget sometimes.
I mean, I know he's not here.
I just forget
we're down to four.

First time,
they told him:
*Don't let there be
a next time.*

Next Time,
he went to juvie.

And the next Next Time.
And the Time after that.

The Next Time After That,
they told him:

*This is your last time in juvie.
You're eighteen now.*

Last time,
they told him:
You can
join the army
or
you can
go to jail.

He told *them*
where to go.

But he went
to Afghanistan.

In a camo uniform
and brown boots.

He sends me pictures
where I can't tell
which one's
him.

CRAMMA'S PILLS

are round
and white
and very
small.

You wouldn't think
they could do
much.

But they can.
Oh yes
they
can.

It's like being
wrapped
in cotton
candy.

And the sun is warm
and golden,
all around
me.

Like I'm floating
in a pool,
but the pool
is
full
of sunlight.

A pool of sunlight.
Warm.
Golden.

And all my worries
     float
       away
         like voices.

And instead of echoes,
I get comfort.

Mom is always working…
    it's
      alright.

Rupert is always sleeping...
    he's
      okay.

My sister is always angry…
    she'll
      get on.

Leo is gone…
    he'll
      come back.

There is nothing
    to worry
      over.

The universe
  has
    got it.

And me?

I
can
just

be.

TEETH

Extras, four.
Had budded
in the very back
of my mouth
like weeds.

Wisdom teeth.

Impacted.

Remove them.

In August,
they cut away
my gums
and yanked
those wise teeth
right out
by their roots.

PAIN

Jaw the
size of my
whole head.

Head pounded.
Mouth oozed.
And bled
and

b
l
e
d.

Sent home with
10 little pills.
Round
and white
and very
small.

I didn't think
they'd do much
and they didn't.

I still felt
all the pain.

I just
didn't
care.

My teeth were gone…
they were trouble.

My jaw ached…
it would heal.

I was in pain…
it would pass.

And it did.

After two days
I didn't need those
round
white
pills

anymore.

I'd taken four.

ITCHING

I can always tell
when I'm coming
d
  o
    w
      n.

It always starts
with the itching.

Some people
get the itching
sooner,
but for me it happens
around the three-hour mark, which means

in another hour
I'll be sober.
Not back at zero—
I seem to dip
a little
lower
than where I started
and I seem to get
crabby-cranky, touchy-testy

and I grind my teeth.

Except the four they took.

HOME AGAIN

Isabella's friend,
the stranger?
Her name is Mia.

I find this out
as she's coming out of my house,
which is
right when I'm going back in.

She tells me
this name of hers.
Makes a point of it.

I expect stink-eye
from Mia
for things Isabella
probably
told her.

But Mia's eyes still shine
bright.
Warm and inviting
like
she really wants to know me,
like
she wants me to like her.

I ignore her.

THE BASEMENT

is where we used to play.
To ride trikes
and play dolls
and house
and trucks
and little animals.

Three of us,
then two, but
now
just
me.

Not dolls
or house
or animals:
music.

I mix it
on my phone.
I'm good, too.
I did the playlist
for our sophomore dance
last year.

What I really want is to
make
the music.
There's free software.
But I'd need a laptop.

Can't write music on my phone.
Can't put any software—
free or not—
on my iPad from school.

Those are the
only computers
I have access to.

For now,
I play
other people's music.
But someday,
I'll play my own.
One day,
they'll play mine.

MY BIG IDEA

Mixing music
gets me in the zone,
helps me forget
that I'm alone
in a house that's overflowing.
I'm growing
up on my own.

And then it hits me:
To Mia I'm a mystery.
She's 14, looking for a hero.
I'm a zero
with a history,
but she doesn't know.

She's Isabella's
best friend.
If she likes me,
my sister can.

Maybe we can save each other
from one another;
make the hate end.

And if that doesn't work,
she can at least tell me
why my sister hates me
so
darn
much.

BTW

I'm not failing school.
Just one class.
Or, maybe two
if you count library day,
which I don't.

Not
anymore.

MRS. SCHILLER

wore
long plaid skirts,
ankle boots,
and cardigan sweaters
over turtlenecks.

She wore her long,
              silver
              hair
                 in a
              l o o s e,
                 messy
                 bun.

Mrs. Schiller looked
like a librarian
should look.

Her blue eyes sparkled
like stars
over her
                 <cat-eye reading glasses>

which she wore
on a chain
around her neck
when she didn't have them
on her face.

But mostly she did have them on.

Because she read to us
a lot.
Because Mrs. Schiller
wanted *us* to read.

All of us,
even the kids who
didn't
couldn't
wouldn't.

She would find you something
to like,
something simple,
something you wanted to read,
even if that meant
you had to
first learn
how.

Or at least get better at it.

I got sooooo much better
that I was placed in AP English.

THE NEW LIBRARIAN, MS. JORDAN

First of all, *Mizz*?
What era is this?
I think women have proved
we mean more than a kiss.

And what's with those pants?
And hiking boots?
Ponytail, high up on her head,
not loose,
and tight sweaters with
pictures of
moose.

She's from Away
not from Here,
not from Maine.

She dresses "outdoorsy"
and tries to talk cool.
But she looks 19,
must have just finished school.
How can she have read
beyond *Winnie the Pooh*?

Now she's
going to tell me
what I'm supposed to do?
What I'm supposed to read?
What books I need?
Mizz Librarian, please!

27

HALLOWEEN

Seventeen is too old
To go out.
You get yelled at.
People shout at you
even if your costume is good,
which mine isn't.
We decided last minute,
Alexis and I.

It's not even about the candy.
We can obvy
buy it from the store.
We'd just like to be
little kids once more.

THE BUS

is a mess,
a test.
I stay at the back
with the rest
of the bad kids
who can't hack it
but I do my homework
while they make racket.

Swagger and bragging
while their grades are
lagging behind.
They'll get defined
as dumb and
made to repeat,
or sent to school
in the heat.

Or end up in camo
with boots on their feet.

They're losers and thugs,
but they leave me alone
so I ignore them,

ignore everyone
until I get to school where there's Alexis.

ALEXIS

meets me,
eyes a-sparkle.

Guess who dropped a new beat?!

    Santa Claus.

Not till December.

    The Great Pumpkin.

Close!

    Oh my God just tell me. <gasp> Wait! No!

Yes!

    Sizzy!?!?

Ah-YUP!

    Candy!!

<I pretend to throw candy at her.
She pretends to eat it.>

We head to home base,
our first class of the day.
When I used to read, I used to like it.

Now that
reading is treason,
I kind of despise it.

> *Think Sizzy*
> *will ever*
> *play*
> *here?*

Nope.
He's
too big
now.

> *But he's from here.*

Doesn't matter.
Did you do the homework?

> *Chemistry yes,*
> *English no.*

She raises an eyebrow at me.
This is
a thing
she can
actually,
physically
do.
And I'm jealous
about it.

Serrrrious? She rolls the R
which is
from Lekker,
another band
we like.
And
is extra funny
because
we're from
Maine
where,
as Sizzy
will tell you,

"R's get skipped like
gym class in middle school."

*What's with
you and English
lately?*

I snarl at her and go cross-eyed.

> *What's with
> *you*
> and chemistry?*

*Chemistry
is way easier
to make up.*

I just laugh
at this.

Not for me!

THE TROUBLE TWINS

That's what
they call us
at school,
me and Alexis V.

What they mean
when they say that
is

Alexis Valcourt   &   Charlotte Navarro
smart
          smart
                    smart
                    trouble
                              trouble
                                        trouble

What they don't know:

How bad Alexis's house stinks
of cat pee,
drunk stepdad,
dirty dishes,
and rotting trash.

How she stays with me
without warning,

just shows up
with her purse and a change of clothes
or sometimes
just a change of underwear.

How the police come
once or twice a month
and take one
or the other
of the adults
away.

How Child Protective Services
has taken
her little sister away
twice.

My mother may never
be home.
My stepfather may never
get out of bed.

But at least they're not
drunk and high and
beating on each other
and throwing
my kid sister
down
     the
       stairs

for wanting dinner.

LUNCH

Hallway fights are usually planned.
But lunchroom fights just happen.

Once a month we have one,
and it's usually a bad one.

It's seldom juniors,
sometimes seniors,
usually sophomores,
or it's freshmen.

Alexis can't stand fighting.
She tries to get the attention
of whoever is about to brawl.
It doesn't work all
the time.
Sometimes she ends up in the middle,
then I have to save her.

Sometimes it's me that's brawling.
She's learned not to try to save me.

NOT MY SISTER

It's Alexis who points her out.
Did your sister cut her hair?
But then the girl
turns around.

Oh that's not your sister.
I thought it was
because
she's wearing your clothes.

And she is!
I mean it's Maine,
everyone wears L.L. Bean boots.
And flannels.
But her T-shirt has a cartoon crow wearing a crown,
and the pants are flared jeans
with a "vintage" checkerboard pattern.
Hand-painted,
I know,
in a studio near Portland
called Bones and Soda.

No one in this school dresses like that.
Except me.
And now,
Mia.

DETENTION

Fighting gets you in detention,
sometimes even suspension,
it doesn't matter if you're smart.
There's an art
to getting out of trouble
Alexis knows it.
I do not.

Same kids every week:
fights, late, mouthy streak.
Bad students, troublemakers,
risk-takers.
We are all always in trouble.
We may be smart but
we can't be taught.

But today
there's someone
different.
A boy I don't know but wish I did.
Really wish I did.

This is the boy
I think about in the bathroom.
This is the boy
I gloss my lips for.
This is the boy
I haven't admitted to liking.
Not even to Alexis.

This is Johnnie C.

He sees me and I freeze.
I look down,
he looks away,
as if to shrug,
as if to say,
Alright I'll let you be
alone.

But that's not what I want.

I still can't move.
It's like I'm caught.
This is my chance,
I'm about to blow it!

And then I see him
take something from his pocket
where he stowed it.

Something
round
and white
and very
small.

And then it hits me—
Johnnie C.
is as scared
as me.

Of course he is,
he's never been here.
I'm here twice a week.

I'm the queen of detention.

I strut right over.
Sit right down.

That little pill,
no water.
He just swallows…

His face goes from mean to normal.
His eyes go from normal to pinpoint,
but also from glassy and scared
to *It's cool, I don't care.*

This is a thing I know,
makes me not scared to say hello.
I'm Charlotte, most people call me Char.

He says, *Johnnie Clark.*
Most people call me Johnnie C.
because there are so many
Johnnies, see?

I smile. *Yes, there are.*

And we talk like this.
Like we are friends or regular people or something.

JOHNNIE C.

is lean (but strong) and tall and blond.
His hair is in his eyes.
His eyes are brown and velvet, like a puppy.

Johnnie C. hunts, fishes, ice fishes, and snowmobiles.
His father owns a lobster pound.
Johnnie's worked at that lobster pound since junior high.

I know
he knows nothing
about me.

What are you in here for? I ask him.

I got edgy with Mr. Davis.

Edgy?

I didn't feel well. I had a flu or something.
Mr. Davis kept asking me the same question
over and over
like I had the answer but wouldn't tell him.

Other people in the class started
to laugh about it,
which made me mad
at Mr. Davis.

Dude, drop it!
I said I don't know.

Finally I told him...
well...

    You told him where to go?

We laugh.
We get shushed.
We take out books and pretend to be studying together.
Which is impossible.

He is in none of my classes. For one thing, he's a senior. For
another, he goes to CTE.

But he thinks up a good one. He says, *Library day?*
It's the one class we might share.

I tell him why I'm there.

    I got edgy, as you'd say,
    with Ms. Jordan.
    Real edgy.

His pinpoint eyes go wide.
You're the girl who—

    Yeah.
    I'm here a lot, I admit.

You fight a lot. I know that.

    I break up a lot of fights and end up in the middle.

I thought that was your friend, Alexandra?

    Alexis. Yeah, her, too.

41

We laugh again.
We get shushed. Threatened with another day in here.

Wouldn't be the worst thing.
And Johnnie C.
WINKS AT ME.

I think I'll die.
But I don't.

CTE

stands for:
Career and Technical Education.

Johnnie goes for construction engineering,
which beats working
at the lobster pound, I'll bet.

He'll get out that way.

My brother Leo went for automotive,
meaning car repair,
which is exactly what he's doing
in the army.

But I guess he got out, too.
In a way.

Somehow, though,
Maine still sends a lot of us
to college.
And if you don't want college?
They set you up for a trade.

Maine tries to take care of its kids.

I wanted to go to CTE,
but Rupert said, *No way.*
You're college bound.
You're smart enough,
you can get scholarships

and you can
get out.

This is how you raise kids
when you live in a mill town
and work in a mill town
and one day
they start
shutting mills
down.

But I didn't argue.
He's probably right.

Besides,
CTE doesn't offer
a program
in music production.

MOST AFTERNOONS

Mia is in my sister's room
when I get home.
Which is also
my room.

Mia says:
We can go somewhere else.

Isabella says:
We're staying here.

I say:
I don't care what you do.

It isn't true.

I STAY

in their way,
deciding
what I want to do.

I figure
I'll just play it cool
until Isabella blows a fuse.

Then I get up.

Mia asks:
Where are you going?

My sister asks:
Who cares?

I just say:
Away.

I LEAVE

Go to Leo's room.

I keep
some pills
in here.

He had
some of
his own.

I leave
them
alone.

His
are not real
Oxy.
At least
they might
not be.

His script
ran out.
There were
none around.
He headed
for Main
Street
in town.

Street drugs
kill.

I take one
of mine
(of Gramma's)
and wait.
Lie on his bed
until that state
of relaxing hits me
and I'm away…

…except today
it's been
20 minutes and
hey,
I still feel the same!

Well, dinner was big.
and I've been really uptight.
Maybe that's why it's not working right.

Probably I need more tonight because
I'm really stressed…
it's Friday tomorrow and there are no tests.
And my homework is done.
So why not take a second one?

I do.

RUMORS

There was a librarian
who swallowed a pill.
I don't know why
she swallowed a pill.
Guess she was ill.

There was a librarian
who swallowed some liquor.
(Oxy is fine, but with liquor it's quicker.)

She swallowed the liquor
to wash down the pill.
But I don't know why
she swallowed the pill.
Guess she was ill.

There was a librarian
who smoked some weed.
She smoked the weed
to chase the liquor.
(Oxy is fine, but with liquor it's quicker.)

She swallowed the liquor
to wash down the pill.
But I don't know why
she swallowed the pill.
Guess she was ill.

There was a librarian
who rode the white horse…

There was a librarian
who rode the white horse...

she's dead,
of course.

LIES

All that stuff they say
about Mrs. Schiller
isn't true.

Obvy!

Liberians
don't do
heroin.

BUT

there are
quieter stories,
too.

About
   operations
and pain prescriptions
   and overdoses
and ambulances
   that came
too late
   to be useful

and so,
   the funeral.

A GOOD EXCUSE

I don't think
those
are true
either.

                    Not
                    deep
                    down.

                And Alexis says
                Mrs. Schiller
                just left town.
                    Moved
              somewhere warm
                    and safe
                down south.

But
those rumors
were
a good
excuse

for
    self-pity
and self-medication
    and memorials
and dedications
    that soothed
right away.

Shooed away
the sadness

and so,
   the habit.

THE HABIT

Brown bottle,
      see-through.
White wrapper
tells you
the contents
and
how many
and
how often.

Six pills,
      nine days.
Then
they were
      gone.
I went to school,
      I carried on.
I went to Gramma's
to help her clean
and
cook with her
and
mow her lawn.

Brown bottles,
      in a row.
I'd forgotten,
      but I know,
Gramma doesn't
take them
but
she bought them.

No,
I didn't
steal them.
I wouldn't
steal
from Gramma.

　　　I asked her:
　　　Why don't you take these?

They make me drowsy,
fog my head.
I only take them
if I can't sleep.

　　　I asked her:
　　　Why do you have so many?

They send them
in the mail.
I don't know
how to
stop
them coming.
Maybe
one day
I'll decide
I'm done.
Ready to go.
I'm eighty-three
you know!
Maybe
one day
I'll just take
all

those
little
pills.

I said
I didn't think
that was
a good idea.

And that maybe
I should
get them out
of her house
so she wasn't
tempted.

And she said:
Okay.

180-some pills—
        nine months' worth!

It was like
Christmas came early.

I left Gramma's
with all
those bottles,

to keep
her
safe,
and keep
me
happy.

HAPPY

means different things
for each of us.

For Alexis,
it means
good grades
and a scholarship
to a music school.
It means
getting away from her mom
and stepdad
and taking
her little sister, too.

For Leo,
it meant doing what he wanted
when he wanted.
I'm pretty sure the army
is the opposite of that.
But…
he smiles
in the pictures he sends.
His emails
are funny.

For Rupert,
I guess
it would mean
getting out of bed.
Or maybe that's
what he'll do

once he gets happy
again.

For Isabella,
I think
it would mean
not having a sister
anymore.

For me,
it used to mean
having a sister.
It used to mean
reading
and talking
about what I read.
It used to mean
"pwning n00bs"
at video games with Alexis.
It used to mean
mixing music
in the basement.

But
HAPPY
has changed.

Now, it means
being
right here, right now.
Floating among the clouds
warm
safe
harmless
weightless.

It means
calm in the storm
that is my household
and my sister.

It means
not worrying,
just for a few hours,
about:

grades
Isabella
Rupert
Mom
Leo
Gramma.
Beating Sinist-Her1 at League of Legends.
Getting a dope mix everyone will love.

For a few hours
every day
I can
just
be.

Even though now
it takes three.

THROUGH THE WALLS

of Leo's room,
when the girls think
I am gone,
like now,
I can hear them
carry on. Chitchatting
the way freshmen do.

Lately
they seem
to be arguing
a lot.

I hear the tone shift
from joking
to mad,
from silly
to
serious.

They fought
about Halloween
before,
whether or not
to go.
(They did.)

There was
some fuss

over the Harvest Dance
and *Why do you like him, ewww!*
(At least they won't fight
over boys.)

But lately,
when they talk,
it's like
they are driving

   down opposite sides
     of the same street:

Isabella says,
Wanna go play outside?

      Mia says,
      Look, have you seen this game?

*Did you figure out
the math homework?*

      *I finished our book for English.
      It's waaaay better
      than that diary one.*

Wanna watch Lewis Stands Up?
*There's like three new ones
you haven't seen.*

      The Bloody
      Christmas Stocking
      *opens Friday,
      we should go.*

Since when
are you
such a reader?
And I liked
the diary one.

Since when
do you
like horror movies?

And
by the way,
what's with those pants?
And those boots?
And that T-shirt?

What are you,
trying to be
    cool?

MIA PUSHES BACK

You should try it, too,
Mia tells Isabella.

I couldn't even get you
to wear lip gloss,
Isabella says.
Now you've got
all this on.

I'm just trying
to…branch out.

You know
who you look like?

I don't look
like
anybody.
I look like me.

And other people
like it.

And why
do you care?

I'm not standing here
telling you
you look basic.

That everybody
owns those same boots
and you should do
something
with your hair.

I like you
how you are.
Why can't you
like me
the same?

I'm kind of proud of Mia.

And

I have the same question.

MOST MORNINGS

Alexis asks,
Where were you?
I texted…

         I was mixing
           till late.
             Then
        I fell asleep.

Sinist-Her1
was playing last night.

Alexis is talking about
an online gamer
we both play against.
Well, we both
used to
play against.

I haven't played
a video game
in more than
a month
now.

She pwned me!
Alexis tells me.
I'm mad about it.
Did you do the homework?

        English yes,
         Chemistry no.

She raises an eyebrow.
You didn't
do the
chemistry?

I snarl and cross my eyes.

Maybe I'm sick
of you
copying it.

I'm not copying.
I'm practicing
how to do it.
I'm learning.

Funny,
your learning
looks just like
my copying.

You want
me to starve!

No?

You want me
to fail,
and failing
leads to starving,
sure as
pot
leads to heroin.

I roll my eyes
so hard
they sprain.

Good thing
I'm not smoking
pot,
I say.

Which makes
me laugh
to myself.
But
I hand over
my
homework
anyway.

ONE MORNING

Chemistry no,
*   English no.*

Alexis
looks at me
very carefully.
Are you,
like,
alright?
Homework
or
homeless,
Char.
Your pick.

I want
to tell her
I'm nowhere near
        alright
actually!

That school
doesn't
interest me.

That
nothing
interests me.

That
I feel
abandoned.

That I still
like reading
but I don't like
talking about
what I read
with anyone.

That Mrs. Schiller was…
not a friend exactly,
but
a mentor.
An adviser.

People
at the
high school
who have
these titles
don't often
live up to them.

Mrs. Schiller
was
"just"
a librarian,
but to me
she
was
like
a counselor.

Then
she left
and didn't even
say goodbye.

This makes me sad
every single day.
So sad that I almost
understand
why Rupert
can't get
out of bed.

But I don't
tell Alexis
these things.

Instead
I laugh
and say:

If I want
to be talked to
like this
I'll text
my mother.

THIS MORNING

(Alexis takes
the chemistry
homework.)

I have news!

                                    Trues?

I might be getting us a gig.

                                    Gig?

DJing!

*There's this crowd
in Ellsworth
throwing these
lit parties
almost
every weekend.*

*Some of the kids
here
go to them.*

                              *Are we
                                going
                        to get paid?*

She sing-chants
a Lekker lyric:

'Course I get paid,
what else would I do
this for?
Making money money money,
gonna even the score!
I'm a rrrrrich chick
hear me roar!

                                        Wicked!

Yeah, so where are you
uploading all these
late-night mixes?
I need demos for the party people.

                                        When?

Like, tonight.
Then, if they like it,
we have to go
to one of their parties.

                                        Have to?

So they can
make sure
they like us.

                          Are we going to like them?

Alexis laughs.

                                But for real, though,
                                        are we?

THANKSGIVING

Mom is at work.
Rupert is in bed.
    Leo didn't call from
        the 7,000 miles
            that he is away.
            Alexis came over,
        but she didn't stay.
Isabella went to Mia's.
At least one of us got fed.

MOST DETENTIONS

are,
if I'm honest,
chill.

I don't
mind them.

We're not
allowed
to talk,

so there are
no fights
in them.

I sit
in the chair
farthest
from the door
and do
my homework,
in this order:
  math
  social studies
  chem
  English.

If I didn't
keep landing
in detention,

I probably
would be
failing school.

The only thing
I don't like
is when I think
about how
I used to stay late
to talk to
the librarian.
And now
I'm staying late
because of
the librarian.

SOME DETENTIONS

Johnnie C.
is in there with me.
The chances
are
one in three.

We talk about
            comedy
            TV
            movies
            buoys
            hunting
            tourists.

He tells me about
            cars
            boats
            lobsters.

I tell him about
            DJing
            gaming
            pizza.

Until we get shushed.

THIS DETENTION

I don't feel good

I'm cranky, angry,
gloomy, and blue.

My head hurts
and my nose is running.

My stomach hurts
and my skin feels funny.

I feel like I'm getting the flu.

So I do something
I never do,
at least
not in school.

>   Three pills
>   and I swallow,
>   wash them down
>   with bottled water.
>
>   Twenty minutes
>   and my head's down.
>
>   'Cause I'm through

feeling sad or
feeling sick or

feeling anything
at all.

I'm sleepy, peaceful,
sunny, and calm.

I feel great.

THIS AFTERNOON

Mia is not in my sister's room
when I get home.

Isabella's anger burns
through her green eyes
and comes hissing
through her clenched teeth:

Mia is listening
to techno.
She used to
listen to alternative.

She's wearing
tall Bean boots.
She used to
wear six-inch Bean boots
She's wearing leggings.
She used to wear jeans.
She wants to watch
horror movies and play video games.
She used to want to watch
stand-up comedians and play outside.

She got an app for her phone
so that she can DJ!

She sounds pretty cool,
I say.

You're stealing my friend!

I blink at her.
Try to blink away
her anger.
It only makes her
fiercer.

Even three pills
can't make
a cloud
thick enough
to protect me
from her.

*You're stealing
my friend!*

I really want her hollering
to end.

I hate you!

So what's new?
I think, but don't say.
I just stand there and take it.

If I were straight I might slap her,
but the Oxy keeps me passive.
Angry, awful Isabella.

Are you done?

She's not…

81

ALSO

today is Mom's birthday.
I'm sure you forgot.
We're all going out to dinner.

> I say,
> *I didn't forget.*
> *I even made her something.*
> *So there.*

But Isabella's face says
she knows as well as I do,
this isn't true.

GETTING READY

I try on:
two pairs of jeans
one pair of pants
one dress.

Char, hurry up. The reservation is for six.

Dinner with my mother
feels like a date.
We never eat together,
she works too late.
Doubles at the mill
since Rupert's layoff.
Never know when your mill
is the next to shut down.

Another pair of pants.
Three tops,
two sweaters, and
another dress.

Charlotte, I will leave you here!

They "laid him off"
rather than "let him go."
Said they were cutting back
even though
everyone seems to agree
it was the RA stuff.

THE RA STUFF

Rheumatoid arthritis…

    beat Rupert up.
        His joints ached and swelled.
        His body rebelled.
    Slowed Rupert down.
        He dropped wrenches and hammers.
        His hands were so damaged
        from the inside.
    Ground him to a halt.
        Hands curled into claws.
        Knees and ankles, too.
            Soon
        all a lost cause.

    Sent Rupert to bed.
        He goes there instead
          of
        to work.

    Rupert's in bed when he used to be
    making us dinner,
    helping us with homework,
going to softball and soccer and school plays.
    Being the Dad my mom married
    to replace the Dad
    she divorced.

This is a thing that breaks my heart.
Every single day.

STILL GETTING READY

The second dress
is okay I guess.
Just need
a sweater
to go
with it.
I know
which one
I want.
But
where
is it?

I think
Isabella's
been throwing away
my clothes.

Or maybe
Mia's
been stealing them.
Who knows?

This makes me laugh and laugh and laugh!

And then I find it,
hanging way
in the back
of my closet

where I used
to keep it
when my mom
first bought it
as a reward
for getting
into
AP English.

Char-lotte! Mav-is! Nah-var-oh!

It's time to go.

ONE LAST THING

I want to function
but also enjoy,
just be.

Isabella is raging,
Rupert seems to be, too.

I already took three,
but I'm still feeling antsy…
one more should do.

And one in my pocket.
Just
in
case.

Rupert's got a script
for Oxy,
also.
I wonder how many he'll take
before we go.

AT DINNER

Mom is weary.
Bleary-eyed and quiet but
trying hard
to smile.

Asking me and Isabella
about school,
about soccer and music,
about Alexis and Mia.

Asking, asking, asking,
but not listening
to the answers.
But she tries,
my mom.

She tries.

She's so pretty, my mother.
I guess everyone thinks that
about their mother.
But I see mine so seldom;
sometimes I forget.

> Mom is always working...
> *it's alright.*

Last year,

> (We come here every year
> for Mom's birthday.
> It's the one day we go
> to a real restaurant.)

Leo sat between
me and Isabella,
even though no one needed to.
Because
last year,
me and Isabella
were still cool.

This year,
Leo is missing.
If I weren't floating on a cotton cloud,
I'd be missing
him.

His lean, lanky self,
his big, boomy voice—
almost always laughing.
Sometimes, too loud.

> Leo is gone...
> *he'll come back.*

This year,
Isabella is pushed
so far away from me
that she's almost sharing
Rupert's chair.

If I weren't floating…
I'd be missing
her, too.

Her dark, curly mane.
Her green, sparkling eyes—
almost always laughing.
Sometimes, in a mean way.

Isabella is always angry…
she'll get on.

This year,
poor Rupert looks
like a walking dead person
on the verge of tears.

He used to be as handsome
as my mom is pretty.

He used to have
two good hands and
two good legs and
a mouth full of perfect teeth
that were so white,
they almost glowed
when he laughed.

He may still have the teeth.
I haven't seen him laugh in so long
that I don't know.

I used to miss him every day,
then just
      most days,
now
      only
every
      other.

Rupert is always sleeping...
he's okay.

THE MENU

The waiter comes and talks and sets menus in front of us.

The letters don't look fuzzy.
But my brain
can't seem to
quite
make words
out of them.

And,
if I'm honest,
I'm not hungry.
I haven't been
in a couple days.

But I don't want to upset Mom.

So when the waiter comes back,

> I ask,
> *What do you recommend?*
> He says something about salmon.
> I say, *Great.*

Rupert scrunches his tired, gray face at me.

Are you feeling alright? he asks.

> *Yeah, why?*

Because you always get the steak.

Yeah, Isabella chimes in, *like always always.*

If I weren't floating...I would
say...
*some*thing.
But since I'm all aglow,
I just shrug.

Rupert looks at me some more.

I'm maybe gonna not eat meat anymore, I say.

My sister rolls her eyes.
Oh, why?
Because that stupid Lekker band
is vegetarian?

For some reason, this makes me smile.
Which makes Rupert frown.

Not his usual
           on-the-verge of tears
frown.
This is different,
like he's concentrating real hard
or looking at something
that doesn't make sense.

Or something
that he doesn't
believe.

Are you sure you're okay?

93

Yes! (haha) *Why?*

Rupert seems to be
paying an awful lot of attention
to me.

I'm just gonna go use the restroom real quick!

BATHROOM MIRROR

is showing me
Me.
But I can't quite see…

I really make my brain focus.
I understand now
what Gramma meant
about "brain fog."

It's nice if you *want* to get lost in it.
But it's a little scary
if you need to, like,
do something.
Even if all you need
to do
is to see

…what they see
when they
see
Me.

LITTLE PILLS

After
they eat
and I
take
a couple bites
but mostly
push food
around my plate,

Rupert goes
to get the car.

Isabella
goes with him.

It's just
me and Mom.

Mom looks
like I feel:

              glowy
  fuzzy   happy
        content

She smiles
at me
over her
still half-full
glass of wine.

Thanks for coming out,
she says.
*It's nice
to see you awake.
I still sneak in
and check
on you girls,
you know.*

(I didn't
know that.)

She puts
her arm
around me,
rubs
my shoulder.

*It's too bad
about this sweater,*
she says.
*I know
it was
one of
your favorites.*

                  *It still is,
                  Mom.
                  You gave me this.*

*I know.
It used to be
prettier
is all.*

It's all
pilled now.

       Pilled?

My heart
skips.

Mom
pulls the cuff
away from
my wrist,
rubs
her thumb
over it.

All these
little fuzz balls?
she says.
That's
"pilling."

All these
little pills
have wrecked it.

I hadn't
noticed.
But now
I see
that it looks

                                    wrecked
                                    worn
                                    tired.

If I weren't
                                              floating,
I know
I'd be sad.

About
the sweater.

About
my mom.

I know
I miss her.

I miss her
having dinner
with us
and watching movies
with us.
And Christmas
is coming.
Who's going
to help us
with the tree?

                        Mom's
                    gone to work.
                Rupert's gone to bed.
                Leopold's gone to war.
                Mrs. Schiller's just gone.
            Where are all the adults in my life?

                            99

And why
are all
these emotions
making it
past
the cotton?

Oh,
and I'm itchy.

So
I'm coming
         D
            O
                W
                   N
    fast.

AT HOME

Isabella walks in
as I'm changing.

She slams
the door,
huffs around.

I'm weighing
my options.
Deciding.

The sound
of her
whining
and slamming
dresser drawers
makes me
want to smash hers
and smash
her mirror too.
Make her stop
acting a fool.

To pill
or not to pill.
That is
the question.

Mom's comments
about my sweater
sound
like a suggestion.
Like maybe
she knows
something
that I think
she doesn't.

Something that
I wouldn't
want her to know,
but maybe
she's discovered…

Isabella
interrupts
my worrying.
*What's up
with you?*
she snaps.
*Rupert's asking
all these
questions.*

*And since when
do you
eat salmon?*

WHY DON'T YOU SHUT UP AND LEAVE ME ALONE!
(Whoa.)
Her eyes go wide
like she's terrified.

Which is how I'm feeling.
I'm reeling!
There's nothing
to decide!

> But it only lasts
> a second
> before she goes
> into a lecture
> about how
> I should be better.

I need a pill
before I kill
my little sister.

> *Do you know*
> *what he asked me?*
> she asks me.

I shove her

> up against the wall.

Maybe you didn't hear me!
Leave me alone!
I don't want you near me!

> Isabella
> shuts off
> the light

with me
still standing
in front of
my dresser.

She throws herself
into bed.
*You don't even
know why
I'm mad.*

And I'm pretty sure

she's crying.

But I'm so

angry
itchy
achy
sniffly
annoyed

that I don't care.

NEWS FROM ALEXIS

They
loved loved loved
your mix!
We're in!

    Candy!

<I pretend to throw candy at her;
she pretends to eat it.>

Then she asks,
Are you ok?
You look
a little gray.

    I'm kind of sick,
    I say.
    Like maybe
    I have
    the flu.

I don't tell her
that I took pills
before
I came
to school.

Just two.

Just to take
the edge off,
get through the day.

Tomorrow
I'll take
one,
then
            none.
I know
it'll be
okay.

                    What
                    do we need
                    to do
                    at this party?

Look cool,
be cool.

                    In other words,
                    show up?

I sure hope
that's enough,
Just showing up.

AT THE PARTY

Alexis made me come.
You know how best friends do.
Now she's gone.

It's not my crowd.
I barely know these kids from school.
I'm wishing I was home.

Tyler lifts a Solo cup.
Mackenzie lifts the stakes.
Two little pills go in her mouth
and two go into Jake's.
Madeline kisses Faith.
They leave the room with Noah.
It's like home:
I'm in a crowded house,
and feeling all alone.

But I see
Johnnie C.
at the same time
he sees me.

Twirl my hair,
gloss my lips,
smile cute,
swing my hips.

And I'm nervous,
like I thought
I might be.

So I take a pill
from my pocket.
Glad I brought it.
(It's not like me.)

Johnnie C.
sees me.

I say,
Don't judge.
Don't knock it

till you
try it.

And he says,

Oh
I
have

and I know.

I know.

I know it.

AT SCHOOL

Alexis says,
He's your boyfriend?
Since when?

                    Since you left me
                            with him!

I went
to the
bathroom!

                    You were gone for an hour.
                    What'd you do, take a shower?

Charlotte,
Alexis says.
He does drugs.

I saw you take his pills.
Saw what they did to you.
Johnnie C.'s got a will
and a way
of making girls
do what he wants.

What Johnnie wants
is me
and what I want
is him.
So, I don't see a problem.

But Alexis looks so grim.

I don't argue
with my best friend.

Don't tell her
that
the pills
were mine.

Like the decision

to end up
in the bedroom.
Smoke some pot
and drink some wine.

That's where
she found us,
where
she dragged me from
before
she took me home.

Where I
crawled
in Leo's
window,

no longer
drunk,
but
still quite
stoned.

I don't argue:
She's a real friend.

Let her think
she's
getting through.

Besides,
her version's easier and
better than
what's true.

FIGHT

Despite my trying to avoid it,
Alexis has this look
that I know better
than to toy with.

It's the look
she usually has
before we fight.

But it turns out
she's just worried about our gig.

It's a New Year's party.

So we've got plenty of time.

Yeah, as long as you use it to practice.
It's a live gig you know.

Oh.
Well it doesn't matter,
I'll be using my phone.
I could pre-record something.
No one would know.

She glares at me.
I kind of feel she's taking this
too seriously.

Four hours is a long time,
given what they're paying us,
which isn't much.

Her glare gets meaner,
This is—

Before she can tell me
what this is,
there's yelling
from
        around
          the
            corner.

MY FAULT

Hollering,
a voice
I know well:
You can go straight to—

       shove
              push
      pull
tug

I told you
my sister was—

And I'm sad
before I see her,

the other girl

I know whose face
will whirl

around to meet mine
and Alexis'.
Know that she
has muscle
but won't flex it.

But worst of all,
I know
this fight

is largely
my fault.

Alexis hollers
in her
Dad Voice:
*What are
we doing here,
girls?*

Because I should
have told Mia
a long time ago,
go away
and leave me alone.
I should
have just
ignored her.

Alexis takes hold of Isabella,
around the waist
from behind.

Isabella lost Mom, too.
And Rupert.
And Leo.
And though she never knew
Mrs. Schiller, she'd heard from me
how cool a teacher can be
and she lost her before
she even got there.

I really wish
I didn't care.
But…

Alexis pulls Isabella away.
My sister's arms
and legs

fly.
She is an animal
wild with sadness.

Isabella doesn't like me
any more than before.
Instead,
she just dislikes Mia
more and more.

I can't be the reason
Isabella loses
her best friend.
This has to end.

MY (WRONG) ANSWER

I grab Mia
around the waist.
Just like Alexis did Isabella.

When Mia turns I see
she's more angry
than scared.
Still, her face lights up
with relief.

I know being kind
or listening to her
will only
make her
like me more.

So I let myself get mad
about her hitting my sister,
make fun of her,
call her a name or two.
And when her lip
finally goes out
and her eyes get glassy
with unspilled tears…

I screw up.

I tell her:

Having a friend
means
being a friend.

Maybe you should be happy
with the friends you've got.
Instead of trying to get more
by changing who you are.

She's looking at me
like how
you'd look at an angel.

She says, *Wow!*
Your sister HATES you
and you're still
sticking up
for her.

A DIFFERENT PARTY

This time without Alexis,
only with Johnnie C.
He's who invited me,
then picked me up
in his older brother's car.
And here we are.

Holy cow,
I can tell you
right now,
everyone here is high.

Not just on Oxy.
That's, like,
a start.
Like the foundation
of a house
of beer and wine and pot.
Plus someone's got
some Adderall.

I think
this is going
to be
too much.
Like last time.

But Johnnie
puts his arm
around
my shoulders
and tells me
not to worry.
Everyone's cool, he says.
And the Oxy
should be kicking in
soon.

And he's right.

AT SCHOOL

Alexis comes
bouncing up to me
like a puppy,
cute and springy.

*Have you been
practicing?*
she asks.

I squint at her,
unsure.

For our gig!

                      Oh, that.
                Not for that
     specifically, I admit.
          But I've been,
              you know,
           mixing, I lie.

Alexis shakes her head.
Just what I was afraid of,
she says.

*We need to plan on
practicing together
as soon as
we can.
How about tonight?*

But I can't tonight.
Because I've got…

ANOTHER DIFFERENT PARTY

Johnnie and I
sit in a giant beanbag chair
in the back
of a living room.

I still don't know
exactly whose
living room.

But we're not too far,
maybe an hour from home.
Still, Hancock Point?
May take only an hour
to get to,
but it is a million
miles
away.

Like,
may as well be
Beverly Hills.

These houses
are mostly owned
by people
from Away—
Boston, New York, Connecticut.

Four-bedroom,
five-bath

mansions
where they live
for a few weeks
in the summer.
Sometimes the whole family
comes for the holidays,
all the siblings
and in-laws.

(Sin-laws, Rupert
used to call them.
Hahaha!)

Probably
the kid
who threw the party
doesn't live here.

Probably
his parents
take care
of this place.

So he has a key.

Johnnie
pulls me closer.
Grins at me,
golden and crooked.

Thanks for the hookup, he says.
He means
about the Oxy.

He was down
to one
pill
so I gave him
some of mine.

I'm running low,
need to go see Gramma
sometime soon.

But I don't feel
like there's a rush,
because I don't plan
to take it that much
anymore.

Just special events.
Like tonight.

ALEXIS, AGAIN

At school.

She comes
up to me
less bouncy,
more cool.

I heard
where you were
last night,
she says.

I know
you have
this boyfriend
and all but…

> *But what?*

I never thought
a boy
would get
between us.

> *Get between us how?*

Listen:
Are you
DJing
this party
with me
or not?

Because if you are,
We need to practice.
To-geth-er!

                                        I want to.
                                          I do!
                                       It's just...

JOHNNIE C.

is easy
to be
around,
quiet and soft and glowing.
I never thought
I'd want
to do Oxy
  with
someone.

                        It's one of
                        my ways
                        to escape.

But Johnnie
makes it
even nicer.

I like how he
kisses me
before the pills kick in.

He comes home
with me
after school
most days now.

We used to
put a chair
against the door

to keep
Mia and Isabella out.

But now we just
sneak into
Leo's room.

Johnnie isn't
planning on
college.

He's not even
counting on his
CTE
to land him
a job.

He figures
he's
army bound.

I tell him
about Leo.
     My brother who is gone.
He tells me about Anthony.
     His brother who
     used to do
     Oxy like we do.
     Then he switched to heroin
     because
     it's cheaper
     and easier to get.

          Heroin?
          That's for addicts!

Johnnie C.
just looks at me.

                              No, I tell him.
                         If it comes to that,
                              I'll just quit.

That's what he said,
Johnnie says
very slowly.
Then he tells me
Anthony
is dead.

THE PARTIES BLUR TOGETHER

Johnny grins
at me,
glowing.

His eyes
are
pinpoints.

I wonder how many angels
are dancing in them?
All of them,
I'll bet.
All the angels
dancing
on the pinpoints
in my boyfriend's
eyes.

And I think
how much I prefer
that
to the look of
meth
or Adderall.
Where the pupils get
huge
and you look like
an alien
or
like you're

having a heart attack
but you
haven't figured
that out yet.

Johnnie is talking.
I think
he has been
but I'm just
suddenly aware of it.

It's HARD
to focus.
I'm TIRED.
Soooo sleepy.
Soooo—

Charlotte?

                                        Wha?

He laughs.

*You maybe
took too much.
You're nodding off
on me, girl.*

I think this
should scare me,
but it doesn't.

It's like
the howl of a wolf

but only
on a television.

Anyway, he says.
*I asked
how much of this
you have.
And would you
be interested
in selling?*

                              Selling what?

He laughs again.
*All this
Oxy
you say
you have
lying around.*

                                        *Oh.
                                     Yeah,
                                whatever.
                                   Sure.
                             If you know
                                someone
                              who wants
                                to buy it.*

MISTAKE №1

Mistakes
don't always
 look
like mistakes.

Sometimes
they look
like

                           winning.

Sometimes
they look
like

                           money.

Johnnie C.
comes back
days after
the

                           party.

He hands me
enough money
to buy
my

                      music software!

If
I gave him
some more
pills,
I
could buy
some decent

                                         headphones!

and maybe even
my own

                                                laptop!

But I gotta stop.

I'm nearly out
and won't see
Gramma
till Saturday.

SURF'S UP

Johnnie says
he hopes
I've got more,
because
he's got
a lot
of buyers.

I ask him
how he knows.

I keep getting texts.

                    I don't like it
                    that people
                 are texting you
                  about drugs!

How stupid
do you think
I am?
I don't text:
        Hey,
        wanna
        buy
        some
        Oxy?

                 Okay. What do you text?

Surf's up!

                                        What?

That's the text I send.
If people
are interested,
they text back:
Hang ten.

Sometimes
they text
"Hang ten"
to me first.

That still seems
fishy.
Being
that we live
in a place with
little surfing.

He laughs at this.

Johnnie says,
You know,
if you
crush it up
and
snort it
you won't need
as much
as when you just
swallow the pills.

How do you know?

*That's what
someone
told me,
anyway.*

*Might
be worth trying
if
you
want to make
some
more money.*

I don't like
the idea
and
I tell him.

To his credit,
he drops it.

HANG TEN

But
I get to thinking
about the money.

The fewer pills
I need,
the more money
I can get,
and the faster
I can get
my DJ stuff.

*You have people
who want this
right now?*

Johnnie C.
waves his phone
at me.

Right this very minute.

MISTAKE №2

Popping pills
wraps you in
a cloud.

Snorting crushed
pills
takes you
        straight to
            heaven.

COMING DOWN

Crashing.
Itching.
Scratching.
Glass shards.
Needle pricks.
Every muscle aching.
Head feels like it's breaking.
Splitting right in two.
Nothing to do

except   another   line.

WAKING UP SICK

Slept 12 hours,
feels like 4.
Woke up with,
like,
the flu.

Again.

Only worse.

Yeah,
I know
what this is.

                    I KNOW.

I need
to see Gramma
and get
more pills.

I'll keep
just a couple
to take
the edge off.

Sell
the
rest.

Then

work on
getting off
this stuff.

GRAMMA

But it turns out
Gramma
is sick, too.
She calls
and says
not to come.
We'll have to
bake tomorrow,
if
she's up to it.

If.

If?

IF SHE'S NOT UP TO IT I'M GOING TO DIE!

WHOA

Okay, calm down.
This is bad, though.

What's in the house?

Go to the bathroom,
shut the door.
It doesn't
feel like
a safe place
anymore.

WHAT CAN MAKE THIS STOP HURTING!?!?

Calm down. Breathe.

THROW UP. HEAVE.

Okay, that's over with...

Feels like
flu.
Take
flu medicine.

WHICH IS IN THE LINEN CLOSET.

It's okay.
I can make it
to the linen closet.

House is cold…empty?
Mom's gone.
Isabella, too.
Rupert? Rupert!

RUPERT

Oxys!
On his
bedside table.

Rupert and Mom's room
is still.
Creep in.
See a mound—he's here, dang!
BUT
on his bedside table
sure enough
is a round,
brown
bottle.

Another step…

What do you need, Charlotte?

Geez!

I jump
about
10 feet!

Uhhhh…
Where's NyQuil?

Really.

Uhm, yeah?
<sniffle>
I have the flu.

<<a
very
long
pause>>

*You seem
to get the flu
a lot lately.*

DO YOU KNOW WHERE THE NYQUIL IS OR NOT?!

Uh-oh.

But Rupert is
very calm.

It's in the linen closet.

So calm.

Where it always is.

It scares me.

*And Charlotte?
That bottle
by my
bedside*

isn't Oxy.

148

It's Humira
for my arthritis.
So don't
take it
or
sell it.

KNOCKED OUT

by the NyQuil.
But wake up
in a cold sweat.
Still tired,
more tired.
Stomach hurts.

ACHES! CRAMPS!

Like it's
tied
in a knot
and
all the food
started to rot
and it's

POISONING ME!

THIS IS CRAZY.

GO SEE GRAMMA
NOW!

TAKE HER SOME SOUP
OR SOMETHING.

And then my phone rings AGAIN.

ALEXIS

Like, the 50th time.

WHAT DOES SHE WANT?!?

But hey!

I pick up.

Can-you-take-me-over-to-my-Gramma's?

I blurt.

Your Gramma's?
She's like,
three blocks away.
And we have to practice.
And what's
          wrong
with you?
You sound
          awful!

                    Practice what?
                    And I have the flu.
                    And I know
                         it's only
                    three blocks.

151

But I don't
feel good
and it's cold
and
you know
what?

Forget it.

I'll call
someone
else.

JOHNNIE

comes to get me.

In his
dead brother's
car.

(Why does this
just hit me
now?)

You're a mess,
he says.

                                        Help me!

Well...
you're going
to see your Gramma,
right?
To get more pills?

                            I CAN'T GO LIKE THIS!
                                        HELP ME!

RELAX!
I just want to make sure
because
I've only got
a few left.
Everyone is dry
right now.

That's how come
I sold all yours
so fast.

ALL!?
HOW COULD YOU SELL ALL
IF YOU—

CALM DOWN.
How many do you need?
I mean
really
need.
To take the edge off?

I dunno, like four?

He gives me
four
little pills.

As soon as
I
see
them,

I
feel
better.

154

BETTER

I try to grind
two of
them up
but I'm shaking
too much.

Johnnie
has to
do it
for me.

I'm quitting after this,
I tell him.

Okay, he says.
Here.

I snort them.
It's like
coming back
from
being dead.

No pain,
no sniffles.

Give me the other two!

Why don't we wait?
I don't have many left.

That should get you
to your Gramma's.

                                    I have to spend,
                                              like,
                                        some time
                                            there.

How much time?
You said she's sick.

                                        I at least
                                have to make her
                                        some soup!

We stop
at Hannaford
and I buy
some
canned soup.

I also get
some cold medicine,
and these
chewy caramel candies
that she likes.

But when we get there,
Gramma
won't let me in.

DEAD

I mean,
she answers
the door.

But she says,
No, don't make a fuss.
Is that your little friend there in the car?
Don't make him wait.
I can put soup
on the stove
for myself.

Thank you
so much
for thinking of me,
sweetie!

I feel like scum.

I give her a hug,
looking around
the living room
as I do.

I ask her,
(try to make it
sound like a joke),

Got any more drugs
you need me to get rid of
for you?

Oh,
I've been meaning
to tell you!

I'm so glad
you took those away.
It made me really
gather up my courage
and tell my doctor that
I needed
something different.

OH

And you know what?

NO

He gave me
something different!

OH

Something
just
for arthritis.
Humira.
It's
not
   even
     a pain pill.

GOD

It's some kind of
"blocking something."
I don't know
exactly.
But it works
much better—
it actually
does something.

I'M

And
it's
   not
      addictive.

DEAD

BETTER OFF DEAD

Johnnie punches
the steering wheel
about
a hundred
times.

                                        crashing

His hands go to his neck,
his arms,

                                        itching

his chest,
his face.

                                        scratching

He punches
the driver's window
and the radio
and the rearview.

                                        glass shards

He tells me,
All
I
can
get
now
is
heroin.

                                        needle pricks

He takes me
by both shoulders

                                every muscle aching

and he shakes me

and yells
right in my face:
*Why'd you lie
to me?*
And he shakes
me some more
and my head
smacks
the passenger
window.

                  head feels like it's breaking

Again
and
again
until I haul off
and punch him in the face.

I
punch
my
boyfriend
in
the
face.

                      splitting right in two

And I tell him:
*Touch me again,
see what happens!*

                          nothing to do

except   get out of   the car.

STUMBLING HOME

Shaking.
Sniffling.
Aching.
Crying.
Dying.

Missing Leo.
Want to blame him,
blame anyone!

Leo!

LEO

Oxys!
Under his
mattress.

Are they
worth the risk
even though
I know
they're street drugs
and dangerous…?

I stand
tiptoed
on the trash can,
shimmy in

to a nightmare.

MIA

Young girl,
    14,
passed out,
not a dream.
Leo's bed.
Is she

                       dead?

Scream
          ScReAm!
                    SCREAM!!!

NO, MIA

Just sleeping.

Now
awake.
     Startled
     but not
     crying or
     shaking.

I take a close look at her.
She doesn't
look stoned.

But
in her hand
is a round,
brown
bottle.

And my moment
of
     worry
     sorrow
     guilt
        gone.

THOSE ARE MINE!

They're Leo's.

WHO DO YOU THINK YOU ARE?!

Well, they were Leo's.
They're mine now.

I fly
at her,

throw her
on the ground,

pry the bottle
from her hand.

> *ARE YOU INSANE!!!*
> *ARE YOU STUPID?*
> *I WILL KILL YOU!*
> *DO YOU UNDERSTAND?!*

> *I*
> *WILL*
> *MURDER*
> *FOR*
> *THIS*
> *DRUG!*

I struggle the bottle open.
There are
only
two.

> Were there
> more
> before?

I need to wait.
Until I
can't wait
        one
                second
                        longer.

        I look
        at Mia
        once more.

                                        What
                        are you doing here?

I just
        wanted
                to try it.

She's
        so
                calm.

I lunge
at her
again,
grab
her by the
shoulders
and shake her
the way
Johnnie
shook me.

I just spent
literally
my whole day
trying
to find Oxy!

I tried
to steal
from my stepfather.

I blew off
and lied to
my best friend.

I was ready
to break into
my grandmother's
house!

I
punched
my
boyfriend
in
the
face.

I'm a
stinking
sweating
sniffling
shivering
MESS.

Tomorrow?

Will be
the same
all over
again.

I glare
into
Mia's
dull eyes.

She grins
stupidly.
Says to me,

You
made
it seem
so
cool.

I say
to her
the most honest thing
I've said
to anyone
since I started
Oxy:

You picked a bad hero.

MY SCREAM

was a siren.

First responder
is Rupert.

SPEAK TO ME

An accident,
but no ambulance.

Rupert knows
who to call.
Calls who needs to know.

Mia is waiting.
I'm pacing—
itchy, angry,
heart racing.

Mia's relaxed.
Me, I'm like a cat
on a hot tin roof.
Like a
hacker
who's been caught
and can't run
any faster.

Finally,
I drop
next to Mia
and just plain
ask her

to please explain

why
my
sister
hates me
soooo
much.

And
to my surprise
she does.

ALL THAT

I've been
sad about,
Isabella
has been
sad about, too.

Isabella *talked*
to Mia.

I kept silent,
tried to hide it…

Everyone is gone.

                                        Mom
                                        Rupert
                                        Leo…

But where
on my list
I have
Mrs. Schiller—
        who read to us,
        talked to us,
        took us seriously,
        protected me,
        counseled me,
        then disappeared—

Isabella is angry
with me.

THE WORST PART

The part that
    stings
most of all

is when Mia says,
through
half-closed eyes,

I think
Isabella started to hate you
when you stopped reading to her.

This makes me feel
like the biggest
failure
ever.

Well.
That is,
        until…

WITHDRAWAL

Bone crushing.

Muscle tearing.

Teeth grinding.

Just

one

pill

PLEASE!!!

Like
the worst
    flu
I've ever had
in my life,
times 1,000.

I want to die.

COLD TURKEY

is what Rupert
calls it.

> *diarrhea*
> *vomit*
> *sweat*

Imodium
Dramamine
Tagamet

He's helping me
get clean.

> *headache*
> *runny nose*
> *body ache*
> *body shakes*

ibuprofen
Benadryl
valerian root
NyQuil

Just like

THIRSTY!

THIRSTY!

THIRSTY!

Gatorade

grapefruit juice

lemonade

THIRSTY!

broth and soup

he had to.

DAY FOUR

I
kinda, sorta
want to eat
something.

Rupert
makes me
peanut butter
on white bread.

He cuts it
into
nine pieces.

I take
three hours
to eat it.

I don't throw it up.

COOL RUPERT

tells me
to move to the couch
while he puts my sheets and blankets
in the coin laundry
in the basement.

When he comes back up
he sits next to me
and says,

Listen:

Not everything
will be perfect
just because
you stopped using,

You need to be strong
enough to deal.
And then,
you need to be
even stronger.

Because
you're
an addict,
Charlotte.

Not using
is not the same
as not being
an addict.

People will always
disappoint
you and
be difficult.

Your mom and I
will sometimes disappoint you
and be difficult.

Because
we want what's best for you.
And we do know best,
even if you think we don't.

And your mom
will sometimes disappoint you
in order to
put food on the table
and keep the lights on.
Sometimes,
that's what love
looks like,

kiddo.

DAY FIVE

Isabella
comes creeping in…

she has been staying
in Leo's room.
I've heard them playing—
her and Mia—
board games and music
and talking.
Thinking, I don't know,
that I can't hear.

She must think
I'm asleep
because
she pulls a chair up
next to my bed.

So I pretend.

I lie still, breath slow
to see
what it is she wants.
What it is she'll do.

What she does is:
        read
            to me.

DAY SEVEN

Alexis!
I'm embarrassed.
Thank God
  I'm not asleep.
  I don't stink.
  I'm not puking.

She looks like
I broke
her heart.

Seeing it
just about
breaks mine.

She says:
I don't know everything.
I just know you took a
    wrong
    turn.
But now you
re-routed.

You're back
on the map.

She gives me
a big bear hug.

Welcome back.

CARD

Alexis tells me
she's got
a card
for me.

Mizz Jordan
gave them
to everyone
in the class.

Only they're not from
Mizz Jordan.

They're from
Mrs. Schiller.

She mailed them
all in one big envelope
addressed
to the school.

She gave us each
the title
of a book to read,
Alexis tells me.
And her email!
She says she wants reports.

We laugh.
    Which feels good,
    feels great!

She moved to North Carolina,
Alexis says.

Her mother
had a hip replacement.
Mrs. Schiller
went down
to help her out,
and ended up
getting a job
just before
school started.

I wonder why
no one told us.
Why we had to
make up fiction
to fill the space
she left.

After Alexis leaves
I open
Mrs. Schiller's card.

But her card to me
doesn't have
the title
of a book to read.

It has
a whole list of them.

COLD MOM

You're grounded, she tells me.
Until further notice.

Alexis can visit
but no one else.
You can go to Gramma's
but nowhere else.

I wanted to take
your phone away.
Rupert talked me
out of that.

She crosses her arms.
When someone looks up to you,
you have a responsibility.

What she doesn't say:
Mia could have died.

Not with her voice,
she doesn't say it.
But her whole body tells me.

Planted feet, crossed arms, tense shoulders,
deep frown, furrowed brow
and those angry, disappointed eyes.

Mom takes a deep breath.
Then her whole body
screams at me:

YOU could have died.
You could have DIED!

What she doesn't say:
First Rupert, then Leo,
now you.

Not to me,
she doesn't say it.
But I heard her crying on the phone.

Standing in my doorway,
Mom's whole body sighs.
Goes from rigid to limp.
Like she's giving up.

Giving up on me?
But she doesn't say,
I'm giving up on you.

She does say,
So you know,
no one is telling Leo.
He's got enough trouble
of his own.

My body tells her, screams it at her:
I'm sorry
I'm SORRY
I'M SO SORRY!!!

That's cool, Mom. That's fair.
I don't want to go anywhere.

186

CHRISTMAS EVE DAY

Gramma
is not angry.
But thinks she should be,
maybe.
Mad or maybe
guilty.
(*They were
my pills,
after all.*)

I go help her
with the baking.
(For real this time.)

The topic comes up.
I change the subject.
Comes up again.
Gramma changes the subject.

Finally,
she makes us tea.
(She's never been
a coffee drinker.)

We drink tea
and eat still-warm
butter cookies.

And she tells me:

Every generation
has its war
and sends its boys,
and now its girls, too.
Sends them home
with a habit.

World War One
was coffee and cigarettes.
Army handed out
those cancer sticks
like candy.

World War Two
was liquor and speed.
Both sides.
Vietnam,
your great-uncle Seth.
Heroin.
And Afghanistan,
well, that's where
those poppies grow.

Some of those kids come home
addicted to pills.

Painkillers
are the army's
new candy.

I'VE KNOWN NO WAR

I'm an addict for no
      reason
      trigger
      war
      excuse.

But Gramma says,
It doesn't matter.
               The habit
is a thing
that can find
any of us.
It   *comes home to roost.*

And I understand
that there's probably a reason
Gramma didn't take
those pain pills.

Even though
some days
her back hurt
so badly
she couldn't get
out of bed.

I hug her.
Hard.
And we both feel
forgiven.

CHRISTMAS DAY

We

are all

here. Well, those of us

not in the army. But Leo

Skyped! We all got to talk to

and see him. There's a tree and a turkey

and some presents. A lot of presents, actually.

Even one to me from Isabella. Mom *does* have to work

tonight, but not until midnight shift. By which time, she says,

You should be in bed anyway. Everything seems kind of perfect.

All is calm,

all is bright.

Until…

HANG TEN

My phone
buzzes.
It's a text.
From Johnnie C.

Who I haven't
heard from
in more than
a week.

It's two words:
Surf's up!

I don't think,
      don't think,
don't think.
Just type

Hang ten!

Thinking now,
though.
Thinking twice
and three times,

as my thumb
hovers over
  <send>

WANT TO KEEP READING?

If you liked this book, check out another book

from West 44 Books:

SANCTUARY SOMEWHERE BY BRENNA DIMMIG

ISBN: 9781538382837

O s m e l

IN THE ORCHARD

In the orchard picking
his last bag of apples
for the day,

Tío Jorge lifts his cap
and wipes his face.

Lines form
around his eyes
as he squints.

Tío has been
working in the orchard
for more seasons than
anyone can remember.

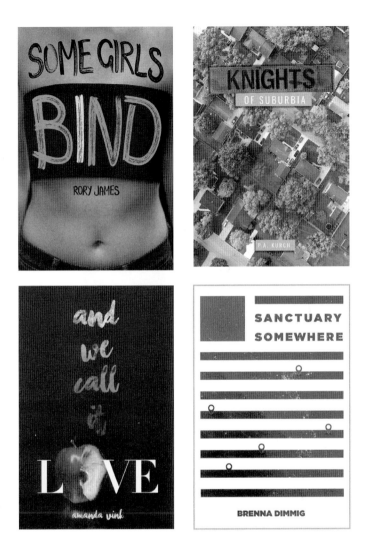

Check out more books at:
www.west44books.com

An imprint of Enslow Publishing

WEST **44** BOOKS™

ABOUT THE AUTHOR

Melody Dodds is a chemist and former substitute teacher. She currently volunteers at a local youth center as a mentor and tutor, and also writes novels and plays. Addiction can shatter the happiest, cleverest, most amazing people we know. Melody wrote this particular book for anyone who has become addicted, or loved someone who did.